Room on the Broom

About the author and illustrator:

Julia Donaldson has written some of the world's favourite picture books. She also writes books for older children, as well as plays and songs, and she spends a lot of time on stage performing her brilliant sing-along shows! Of all Julia's characters, she believes the witch is most like her — but only one of them can fly a broomstick!

Axel Scheffler is a star of children's illustration and has many books to his name which are popular all over the world. Axel wouldn't want to travel with the witch on her broomstick as he'd be too worried about getting airsick.

For Natasha, Sabrina and Jasmine – J.D.

First published 2001 by Macmillan Children's Books
This edition published 2013 by Macmillan Children's Books
a division of Macmillan Publishers Limited
20 New Wharf Road, London N1 9RR
Basingstoke and Oxford
Associated companies throughout the world
www.panmacmillan.com

ISBN: 978-1-4472-3526-2

Text copyright © Julia Donaldson 2001
Illustrations copyright © Axel Scheffler 2001
Moral rights asserted

2 4 6 8 9 7 5 3 1

A CIP catalogue record for this book is available from the British Library.

Printed in China

Room on the Broom

Julia Donaldson

Illustrated by Axel Scheffler

MACMILLAN CHILDREN'S BOOKS

The witch had a cat
 and a very tall hat,
And long ginger hair
 which she wore in a plait.
How the cat purred
 and how the witch grinned,
As they sat on their broomstick
 and flew through the wind.

But how the witch wailed
 and how the cat spat,
When the wind blew so wildly
 it blew off the hat.

"Down!" cried the witch,
  and they flew to the ground.
They searched for the hat
  but no hat could be found.

Then out of the bushes
  on thundering paws
There bounded a dog
  with the hat in his jaws.

He dropped it politely,
    then eagerly said
(As the witch pulled the hat
    firmly down on her head),
"I am a dog, as keen as can be.
    Is there room on the broom
        for a dog like me?"

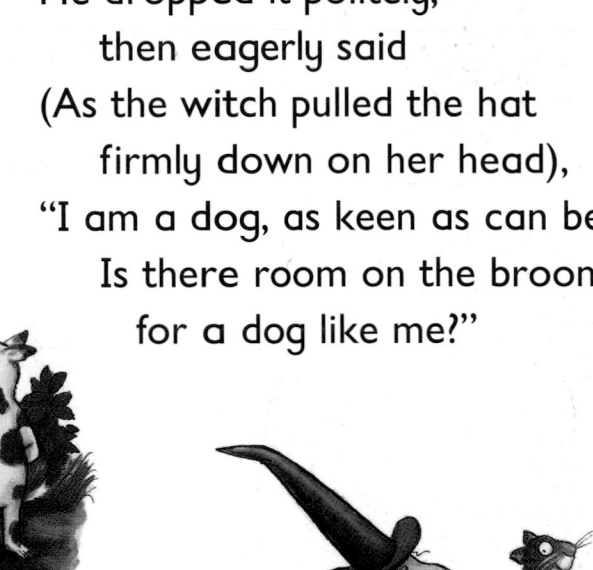

"Yes!" cried the witch,
    and the dog clambered on.
The witch tapped the broomstick and
    whoosh! they were gone.

Over the fields and the
  forests they flew.
The dog wagged his tail
  and the stormy wind blew.
The witch laughed aloud
  and held onto her hat,
But away blew the bow
  from her long ginger plait!

"Down!" cried the witch,
    and they flew to the ground.
They searched for the bow
    but no bow could be found.

Then out from a tree,
    with an ear-splitting shriek,
There flapped a green bird
    with the bow in her beak.
She dropped it politely
    and bent her head low,

Then said (as the witch
    tied her plait in a bow),
"I am a bird,
    as green as can be.
Is there room on the broom
    for a bird like me?"

"Yes!" cried the witch,
    so the bird fluttered on.
The witch tapped the broomstick and
    whoosh! they were gone.

Over the reeds and the
    rivers they flew.
The bird shrieked with glee
    and the stormy wind blew.
They shot through the sky
    to the back of beyond.
The witch clutched her bow
    but let go of her wand.

"Down!" cried the witch,
    and they flew to the ground.
They searched for the wand
    but no wand could be found.

Then all of a sudden
from out of a pond
Leapt a dripping wet frog
with a dripping wet wand.
He dropped it politely,
then said with a croak
(As the witch dried the wand
on a fold of her cloak),
"I am a frog, as clean as can be.
Is there room on the broom
for a frog like me?"

"Yes!" said the witch, so the frog
bounded on.
The witch tapped the broomstick and
whoosh! they were gone.

Over the moors and the
mountains they flew.
The frog jumped for joy and ...

. . . THE BROOM
SNAPPED IN TWO!

Down fell the cat and the dog
    and the frog.
Down they went tumbling
    into a bog.

The witch's half-broomstick
    flew into a cloud,
And the witch heard a roar
    that was scary and loud . . .

"I am a dragon, as mean as can be,
And I'm planning to have WITCH
    AND CHIPS for my tea!"
"No!" cried the witch,
    flying higher and higher.
The dragon flew after her,
    breathing out fire.
"Help!" cried the witch,
    flying down to the ground.
She looked all around
    but no help could be found.

The dragon drew nearer and,
    licking his lips,
Said, "Maybe this once
    I'll have witch without chips."

But just as he planned
   to begin on his feast,
From out of a ditch
   rose a horrible beast.
It was tall, dark and sticky,
   and feathered and furred.
It had four frightful heads,
   it had wings like a bird.
And its terrible voice,
   when it started to speak,
Was a yowl and a growl
   and a croak and a shriek.
It dripped and it squelched
   as it strode from the ditch,
And it said to the dragon,
   "Buzz off! —
   THAT'S MY WITCH!"

The dragon drew back
    and he started to shake.
"I'm sorry!" he spluttered.
    "I made a mistake.
It's nice to have met you,
    but now I must fly."
And he spread out his wings
    and was off through the sky.

Then down flew the bird
    and down jumped the frog.
Down climbed the cat,
    and "Phew!" said the dog.

And, "Thank you, oh, thank you!"
the grateful witch cried.
"Without you I'd be
in that dragon's inside."

Then she filled up her cauldron
and said with a grin,
"Find something, everyone,
throw something in!"

So the frog found a lily,
the cat found a cone,

The bird found a twig
and the dog found a bone.

They threw them all in
and the witch stirred them well,
And while she was stirring
she muttered a spell.
"Iggety, ziggety, zaggety, ZOOM!"

Then out rose . . .

. . . A TRULY
MAGNIFICENT BROOM!

With seats for the witch
    and the cat and the dog,
A nest for the bird and
    a shower for the frog.

"Yes!" cried the witch,
    and they all clambered on.
The witch tapped the broomstick and
    whoosh! they were gone.